GIRAFFES CAN'T DANCE

To my cousins at Sandbanks - Giles
For Fi, John, Rod and Andy - Guy

Also by Giles Andreae
Rumble in the Jungle   978 1 86039 660 1
Commotion in the Ocean   978 1 84121 101 5
Farmyard Hullabaloo   978 1 84121 563 1
Dinosaurs Galore   978 1 84362 609 1
ABC Animal Rhymes For You and Me   978 1 40830 680 2
The Lion Who Wanted to Love   978 1 86039 913 8
Love is a Handful of Honey   978 1 84121 561 7
There's a House Inside my Mummy   978 1 84121 068 1
Nat Fantastic   978 1 40830 317 7
I Love My Mummy   978 1 40830 957 5

ORCHARD BOOKS
338 Euston Road, London, NW1 3BH
Orchard Books Australia
Level 17/207 Kent Street, Sydney, NSW 2000
978 1 84121 565 5
First published in 1999 by Orchard Books
First published in paperback in 2000
Text © Purple Enterprises Ltd, a Coolabi company 1999 **coolabi**
Illustrations © Guy Parker-Rees 1999
The rights of Giles Andreae to be identified as the
author and Guy Parker-Rees as the illustrator of this work
have been asserted by them in accordance with the
Copyright, Designs and Patents Act, 1988.
A CIP catalogue record for this book is
available from the British Library.
34 36 35
Printed in China
Orchard is a division of Hachette Children's Books, an Hachette UK company.
www.hachette.co.uk

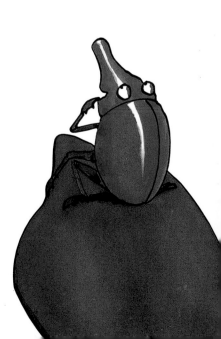

GIRAFFES CAN'T DANCE

Giles Andreae

illustrated by Guy Parker-Rees

ORCHARD BOOKS

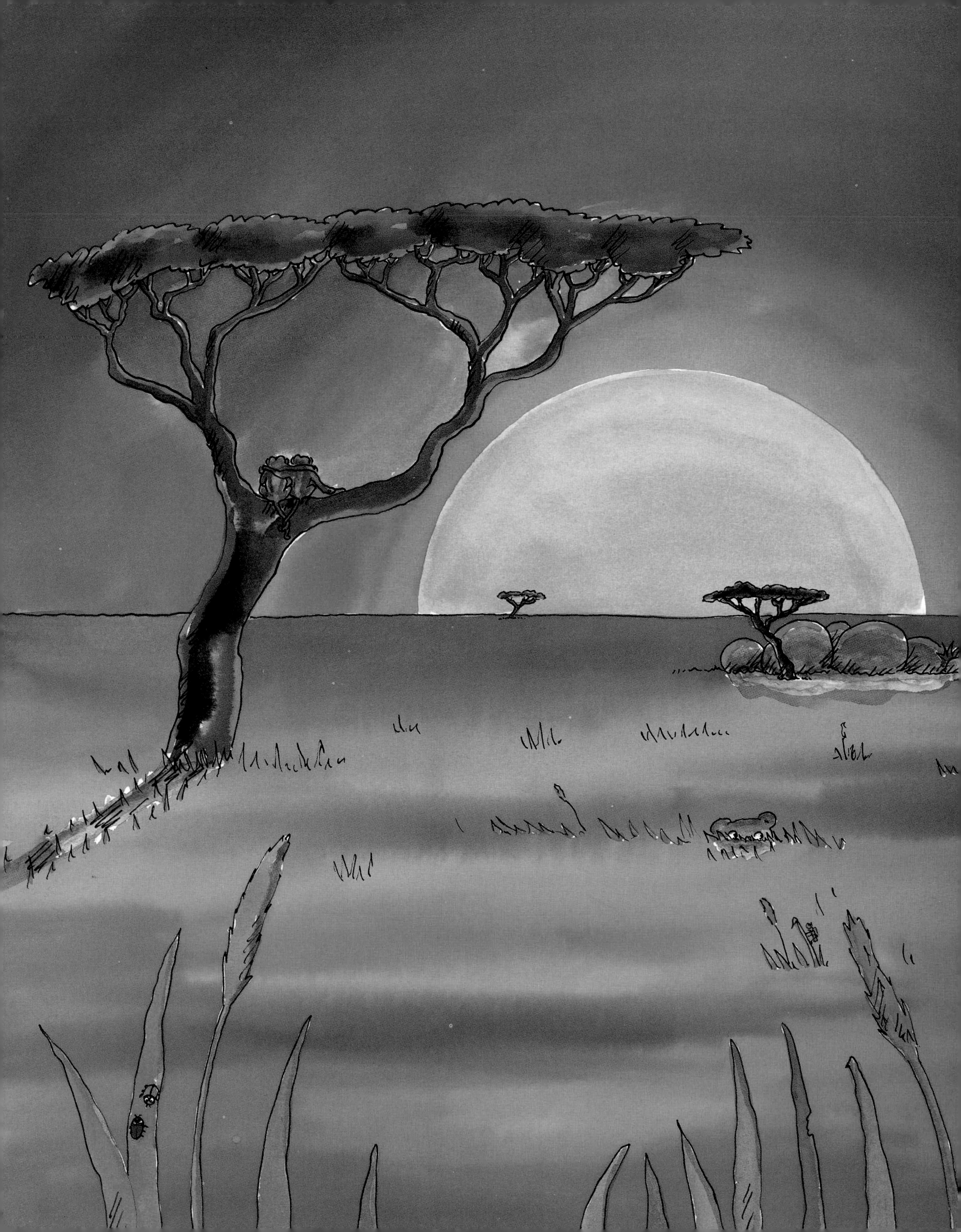

Gerald was a tall giraffe
Whose neck was long and slim,
But his knees were awfully bandy
And his legs were rather thin.

He was very good at standing still
And munching shoots off trees,

But when he tried to run around

He buckled at the knees.

Now every year in Africa
They hold the Jungle Dance,
Where every single animal
Turns up to skip and prance.

JUNGLE DANCE

And this year when the day arrived
Poor Gerald felt so sad,
Because when it came to dancing
He was really very bad.

The warthogs started waltzing

And the rhinos rock 'n' rolled

The lions danced a tango
Which was elegant and bold.

The chimps all did a cha-cha
With a very latin feel,

And eight baboons then teamed up

For a splendid Scottish reel.

Gerald swallowed bravely
As he walked towards the floor,
But the lions saw him coming
And they soon began to roar.

"Hey, look at clumsy Gerald,"
The animals all laughed,
"Giraffes can't dance, you silly fool,
Oh Gerald, don't be daft!"

Gerald simply froze up,
He was rooted to the spot.
"They're right," he thought, "I'm useless,
Oh, I feel like such a clot."

So he crept off from the dancefloor
And he started walking home,
He'd never felt so sad before
So sad and so alone.

Then he found a little clearing
And he looked up at the sky,
"The moon can be so beautiful,"
He whispered with a sigh.

"Excuse me!" coughed a cricket
Who'd seen Gerald earlier on,
"But sometimes when you're different
You just need a different song."

"Listen to the swaying grass
And listen to the trees,
To me the sweetest music
Is those branches in the breeze.

"So imagine that that lovely moon
Is playing just for you,
Everything makes music
If you really want it to."

With that, the cricket smiled
And picked up his violin.
Then Gerald felt his body
Do the most amazing thing.

His hooves had started shuffling
Making circles on the ground,
His neck was gently swaying
And his tail was swishing round.

He threw his arms out sideways
And he swung them everywhere,
Then he did a backwards somersault
And leapt up in the air.

Gerald felt so wonderful
His mouth was open wide,
"I am dancing! Yes, I'm dancing!
I AM DANCING!" Gerald cried.

Then one by one each animal
Who'd been there at the dance
Arrived while Gerald boogied on
And watched him quite entranced.

They shouted, "It's a miracle!
We must be in a dream,
Gerald's the best dancer
That we've ever ever seen!"

"How is it you can dance like that?
Please, Gerald, tell us how."
But Gerald simply twizzled round
And finished with a bow.

Then he raised his head and looked up
At the moon and stars above.
"We all can dance," he said,
"When we find music that we love."